For Someone Special

_By_

Yogesh Sharma

Prologue

"Neither are books for time-pass, nor is the Love we share."

This book revolves around **teenage love** and how two people, **Aarav** and **Arushi**, explore their lives through love. How they find something new in their **relationship** to overcome their extraordinary **feelings** for love. Each poem and short story is about love and the hold it has on all of us.

You are sure to find a poem that will remind you of your own feelings of unconditional love.

Acknowledgement

Thanks to Gauri Sharda for giving your precious time to correct my errors and mistakes.

Thanks to HS for capturing a special moment for my book cover.

Thanks to my Mom, my sister Neha, my friends and all near and dear ones.

And of course, a special thanks to the person who became my inspiration and without whom I could not have written this book.

And a BIG Thanks to all my readers for taking out time to read this and being a part of this beautiful journey.

"for someone special"

Table of Contents

How I Met Her

Mathematics has always been about solving problems, and honestly, I've never been good at either. It was nice to me in my primary classes, but the addition of algebra and trigonometry took it further away from my understanding.

During one of my math classes, when the teacher was asking some basic questions of algebra from the students, I was playing hide and seek with her, trying to avoid eye contact.

"No", not me! Please! Ma'am please, not me, please, look there, ask him or ask her.

But as *luck* would have it, she pointed at me and asked, "Aarav, what is minus into minus $(- \times -)$?"

My mind went blank, my ears became hot, I started sweating and for a moment, I completely froze.

The answer is plus $(+)$ and it was simple. But due to my non-functioning brain, I was unable to figure it out. The jerks sitting behind me murmured (minus square). Without thinking, I repeated it out loud.

And suddenly, the whole class was laughing at me.

However, in a class of 35 students, there was one student who outshone them all. She had a grin on her beautiful face. I can't forget her big blue eyes looking at me like I was *crazy!!*

Then teacher corrected me and at the age of 14, I felt ashamed for not answering such a simple question! But at the same time, I had a feeling that I would willingly do it again just to see that beautiful smile. Until then, I did not even know her name and yet, the only thing I was sure of was that I had a crush on her.

Days progressed.

The first thing I did was to find out her name. *"Arushi"*. Wow! What a sweet name. I started observing her. From her impeccably ironed uniform to her long hair and her yellow headband, everything seemed to draw me towards her even more. She remained quiet most of the times, minding her own business. She was calm, sweet and extremely intelligent. She was the *pixie dream girl* for anyone. I would try to sit next to her in class. During breaks, I got some time to talk to her and she would always help me with the class work whenever I got stuck.

Overtime, I fell in love with her and eventually decided to confess my feelings.

Coincidently, her birthday fell on the day of our Annual Function and I had prepared a little gift for her. I packed a big chocolate bar and wrote a poem on its wrapper.

When the day arrived, I couldn't muster up the courage to actually walk up to her to give the gift. All types of thoughts were going through my mind. What should I do now? Should I simply put the gift under her desk? But what if someone stole or discovered my gift? So I decided to take some risk and discreetly kept the gift in her bag during the lunch break. Yes, I know it was a pretty stupid idea, fiddling with a girl's bag, but it was the only one I had. The bell rang, indicating the end of the break. She came back and my heart began beating faster. I felt like an idiot. What would I have even said to her? *"Hey, I opened your bag while you were not around because I just couldn't gather up the courage to simply hand it over to you"*. No, thank you.

I remember the expression of her face while opening the gift. Her eyes became bigger, her cheeks became red. For a moment, I was afraid that she might get upset but I was lucky she didn't even mind, well, it was her birthday.

After the function got over, she came up to me and handed me back the packed gift saying something like, *"thanks but I can't accept it"* and walked away.

I blinked back the few tears that had come as I sat down on a bench nearby. However, when I opened the package, I found out that though the chocolate bar was still there, she had kept the wrapper. I jumped up from the bench. I wanted to start singing on top of my lungs. My joy knew no bounds. I walked back home happy with a big smile on my face.

Today, after 15 years, we are getting engaged but even to this day, I can't forget my first proposal to Arushi.

Love You Dear!

Do you want to know what I wrote on the chocolate wrapper? Read it below:

"I will brush your teeth,

I will brush them every day,

As you twirl in dresses of lace,

I will wash your face,

I will comb your hair in every sexy way,

I will do your makeup,

I will do anything to brighten up your day.

I will match every step of yours.

Let me walk,

I will walk with you

Even if there are too dark & narrow ways,

I will do take care of your heart,

Will you accept my love

And stay with me always?"

Perfect Selfie Shot

I started dating Aarav six months ago. We had felt an instant connection as soon as we met and were soon *head over heels* in love with each other.

Overtime, non-stop texting and hearing his voice every morning had become an addiction. I often visited his place on weekends. He stayed in a rented apartment in New Delhi, which coincidently happened to be really close to my place. Waking up in his arms made me feel so content. We cuddled, kissed and had a good amount of fun in the bedroom, living up to each other's fantasies.

A few months down the line, my office took us for a two-day offsite to Jaipur. I had promised Aarav I would keep in touch, but poor signal and having my colleagues constantly around kept me distracted the whole day. The only free time I got was at night. I called him up and he sounded furious. He claimed to be worried, but his aggression really annoyed me. Without saying a single word, I *hung up*.

A few minutes later, after introspecting, I realized maybe he was missing me or he was worried because of which he had acted like that. Upsetting him was never my intention and so, I was feeling miserable.

What should I do?

Call him and say *sorry*? Tell him that I love him?

Then an idea struck my mind. A beautiful *selfie* might work its magic.

I set out to click the most fabulous pictures for my love but soon after, realized the truth. I am not very photogenic and I didn't have any prior experience of clicking selfies from some strategic angle either. I was devastated thinking that such a good idea was going down the drain.

I contemplated my options and ended up in front of the bathroom mirror, wearing yellow pajamas and a pink tank top. I had locked the door.

"So here goes nothing." I thought to myself.

Holding my breath, as my heart skips a beat, I tried to copy what I see other women do but still, my poses look so fake. I held the camera closer to my face. Should I angle it from above?

Click.

Should I try something with my curves? How about a hand high on my hips or a popped knee or crossed legs?

Click. Click. Click.

One selfie while winking and another with a duck face and the sign of peace.

Click.

I seem to be getting better at this.

 Where is my lipstick?

A selfie after putting some lipstick on my lips, smiling wryly, arching my eye brows into upside-down V's. Perfect.

Click.

Being so lost in the art of selfie-clicking, I almost forgot the purpose in hand, until my phone rang. The name Aarav highlighted on it.

"Arushi, I am sorry."

He told me exactly what I was thinking that he missed me and really wanted to see me soon.

His words managed to melt my heart, so I instantly forgave him. We continued talking.

It was midnight by then and things were getting hot between us. He was texting me about things he would do to me if we were together at that moment. My colleagues were fast asleep and things were getting really intense between Aarav and me. In the middle of the conversation, he asked me to send him a nude selfie. For a second, I was shocked. I told him I didn't mind sending a selfie, but I won't send a nude one. He kept asking again and again, but I stood my ground. After some arguments, he agreed for a simple selfie.

I selected one from those I had clicked earlier but as soon as I hit the 'Send' button on *Whatsapp,* my phone's battery dies.

By the time I found my charger and turned my phone back on, the spark had already died. I texted Aarav soon after, but he didn't reply. I thought he must've gone to sleep.

The next morning, I didn't receive any text from him. In fact, I didn't hear from him the whole morning. I kept waiting for his call or text and it made me anxious. My heart felt hollow.

We were about to leave the hotel. Standing in the lobby, I tried calling him one more time but to no avail. I crumbled and started crying.

"Arushi!"

His voice reached my ears. My eyes went up in surprise. I turned around and saw Aarav was standing across me. I rushed into his arms and cried fiercely. I held me back tighter and started stroking my hair.

"I was missing you so badly and after what had happened last night, I couldn't control myself. I came here to meet you. I hope you don't mind it." He said to me, softly.

I blushed through my tears and kissed him. I was so touched at that moment. He was there just to meet me. We went for dinner date later that night and eventually, all this ended up adding to our long list of memories.

"One selfie, two selfie, three selfie, four

Let me first shut the door

You need the perfect place for the perfect selfie shot,

Should I stand in front of the mirror or not?

Why need makeup

When the face is already so bright

Try looking natural, making some funny pose,

Blink the eye or play with the nose.

Spread a wide smile, or

Cuddle the teddy tight,

The sexy pout wrapped with some love dose,

It is all a setup for the perfect selfie shot."

A Rainy Evening

It was around the end of June and that day, it was raining heavily. In the evening, when I came out of my office, I was completely drenched. Riding my motorcycle and having the rain drops hit me made me feel so relive. All day's tiredness washed away and it lifted my spirits. I felt so happy within.

As I was driving, I saw her at one of the deserted bus stops that comes along the way. I felt mesmerized by her beauty. I stopped my bike and stood frozen there.

She was standing below the bus stop, trying to save herself from getting wet. But *God was cruel* today, for her and for me too. The bus stop's shed was broken and water drops leaked from there. All of her efforts for keeping herself dry failed. All of my efforts for keeping my heart intact failed as well.

It was *'Love at first sight'*.

It is a feeling anyone who hasn't been at that place can never decipher. Nobody can do justice to it, trying to describe it. I was a well beyond the world type of feeling. It elates you and makes your insides come alive.

She was trying to still hide away from the rain, looking here and there, sometimes wiping her face or drying her hair. Everything looked so picture perfect. I could not take my eyes off her. I wanted to protect her from the rain, to ensure that not even a single drop touches her fair body. I wanted to wipe the water drops from her cheeks, her lips, her eyes. I wanted to see her face clearly.

Standing there, it felt as if God had created her just for me. This feeling of love is so different.

Should I just go and put my hands over her head to save her from the falling rain drops?

Oh, that would look so lovely. I didn't even realize that I actually raised my hand in the air. The rain started hitting my hand hard. But I felt good, I was protecting her. I closed my eyes. I felt her come near me, the feeling of her wet body coming so close to me made me shiver. My hands are still above her head, my heart still beating beyond my control and my breath becoming heavier and faster with every passing moment.

I felt deeply in love with her. I didn't want to open my eyes. The feeling of love is so good.

Suddenly, a loud horn blew near me, making my eyes snap open. There were around seven or eight boys on their bikes, honking again and again loudly. They had blocked her path, getting off their bikes and then tried to grope her. She squirms and tries to get away from them but then, one of the boys held her arm and dragged her towards his friend. She tried to hit one of them but they overpowered her and pushed her on the road. She was struggling to escape as the *'gang of goons'* groped her and tried to pull off her clothes.

She was screaming and shouting loudly, *"Save me! Save me! Save me from these rascals."*

How dare they to touch my love? How dare they try to molest my angel? Without wasting any more time, I shouted angrily and jumped into a fist fight with one of the guys. Another intervened and a scuffle broke out. They were seven in total and the more I tried repelling them from my girl, the more intense the situation became. After a tough fight with those bastards, eventually I overpowered them. The assailants fled quickly on their bikes.

The rain stopped. She was still there, lying on the road. I looked at her and offered my hand for support. She took my hand and stood up.

"Hi, I am Aarav."

"Arushi", she replied with a smile on her face.

"Thank you for saving me from those guys. Thank you so much." She added, her eyes almost welled up.

I also gave her a sweet smile and replied, *"It was my duty to save you."*

We shared our contact numbers and from that day, we become good friends.
After a few weeks of getting to know each other, I finally confessed about my feelings for her. I had written a poem to propose her. She had accepted my proposal and we got married after a year and a half.

"Hey, Ms. Beautiful!

You make my life so colorful,

Your cute little face,

Along with the way you stroke your hair,

Always makes my heart race.

The taste of your lips is so pure,

Send me into a state of bliss for sure.

No one else in the world could even compare,

You're perfect and so is the love we share.

Hey, Ms. Beautiful

Promise to love me always?"

The Proposal

Exactly a year ago, on 7th February, was when Arushi and I met for the first time and today I'm going to mark this day down our history by proposing to her. I was imagining the complete *Bollywood style proposal;* she would gasp, and cry, but then smile and say yes. I wanted all of it to be perfect for her. I had bought a beautiful gold ring studded with a pink diamond.

I couldn't sleep the whole night in anticipation of her reaction. How will she feel? What will her facial reactions be? Such questions kept floating in my head.

I believe that a proposal of marriage is the most romantic moment for a couple to share. It's the moment you say *'I choose to be with you forever. I want to commit to you forever. No one will ever make me as happy as you do. For me, you are the one'.*

We met according to our plan at the National Zoological Park in New Delhi, India. We saw the lion, elephants, deer, a family of white tigers, a jaguar, birds and snakes. Arushi was a committed animal lover and after visiting the zoo, she described it as one of the best of our days spent together.

"Aarav, *it was perfect!*" She said with the most beautiful smile on her face.

Those animals brought a smile to her face and these words, a smile to mine.

We had our lunch in nearby restaurant after which we decided to go to the Qutab Minar. After strolling around for a little while, I decided it was time to pop the question. In front of the historical monument, I got down on my knee and dug through my blazer pockets (to get the ring box). Arushi was giving me an *incredulous look;* her eyes seemed to have grown bigger. Finally, I located the box and offered her to open it. She started jumping up and down in excitement. She opened the box and her smile vanished. She turned and looked at me. I was still down on one knee but this time laughing with tears running down my face. Instead of the ring, this one just had a toffee in it. She tried to hide her smile but failed miserably. She tried to fake her anger. The anger made her look even more gorgeous.

"Aarav, what was this?" She asked and turned her back to me.

"Arushi, look at me." I said to her, softly.

"*No!* You are *mean*."

"*Please, my love*"

She turned and gasped. I had another box (this time the actual one with the ring) in my hand. I held her hand in mine and told her and how much I love her and that I want to be with her forever. Tears of joy gathered in the corners of her eyes as I slid the diamond studded gold ring in her finger. We embraced in a way that was so warm, true and pure that it seemed to join our souls in this moment of ecstasy.

It has been more than 15 years. We are married now and still laugh together whenever we remember this day. This is what I wrote for the marriage proposal.

"I want to shower you with love till the end of my life.

Will you marry me and become my wife?

You are the only one

Always,

Running in my mind.

Such a gorgeous smile adorns your beautiful mind.

Whenever I look deep into your eyes

Your soul shines and my feelings arise

I will give you the key to my heart,

Promise me,

You will protect my love,

Until death do us apart.

We will reunite in the heaven

Whether it's our first birth

Or it's our last."

The Wind

A year into Arushi and Aarav's marriage, Arushi's mother died and with this tragedy, the euphoria of the love marriage ended.

It all happened suddenly and terribly. She died of an unknown disease, a disease which had targeted her mind and controlled her biorhythms and appetite. There was a huge fall in her weight and along came the inability to walk, talk or do much of anything. Past records show that anybody with this disease dies within a year or two of developing the disease.

It was around a year later, while they were still recovering from the shock and mystery of her mother's death, when they found out that the disease had been genetic. After conducting some tests, they found out that Arushi was suffering from the same. Both of them were broken, their lives felt completely shattered.

They had had so many plans, how they will explore the world, build a family, give their contribution in

the upliftment of society together, among others. Now, everything came to a standstill.

But instead of being dejected by the disease, they decided to fight it.

Although neither of them had any knowledge about biology or pathology, Aarav being an engineer and Arushi a commerce graduate, they left their jobs and started taking biology classes. They immersed themselves in contacting and meeting with people working in this field and reading everything about the disease. They worked hard day and night, learning about the disease. Soon, they landed jobs at the reputed Research Centre in New Delhi, India and started working on the antidote of the disease.

Overtime, Arushi's health got worse. By then, they had successfully completed some experiments of the antidote vaccination on animals. They had completely dedicated their lives for finding a cure to this disease. They had finally sent their antidote for government approval.

Things were getting better.

One day, their life took another turn! Arushi had a severe attack. Aarav took her to the hospital.

Arushi was laying there, so *frail and weak*, as if she were ready to fall into a deep, peaceful slumber.

Aarav sat down on her bed and said, *"Hold on, love, very soon we'll get the approval for the antidote and celebrate the New Year together. It'll be a celebration for our new life. You're my elf!"*

Arushi looked up into Aarav's eyes and asked, *"'I am?"*

"Of course." He said, while planting a kiss on her forehead.

She tried to sit up on the bed but couldn't. A tear escaped her eye.

"They say I'm going to die."

Trying to hide his own tears, Aarav replied, *"No, you will not."*

"I love you." Arushi said, holding Aarav's hand in hers, for what it felt like was the last time.

"No!" Aarav said, tears running down his face.

Arushi tried to sit once again. Aarav gave her support. She hugged him very tightly.

She said one more thing, *"I do not want any other person in this world to die because of this disease."*

Aarav wrapped his arms around her and said, *"No one will, we will help them all."*

Silence surrounded then. She died. She died peacefully, in Araav's arms. Aarav sat there like a statue, still clutching onto her body.

Suddenly, the door of the hospital ward opened. It was *Gauri*, Arushi's lab assistant.

"Sir, you will feel glad to know our antidote got approval from the ministries. Both of yours hard work has finally paid off. Now no one will lose their dear ones because of this horrible disease", Gauri said.

Aarav looked up in the air, his face completely wet.

"The wind blows, the wind speaks,

It makes a strange noise.

Wind is the messenger,

That carries your voice.

The wind whips, the wind whooshes,

It whispers in the dark night.

The wind is my only friend,

It stays with me in your place for rest of my life.

The wind hugs, the wind kisses,

It makes my emotions come alive,

Be my wind!

Without you, I cannot survive."

The Attack

After the end of our college, our group planned a trip to Nainital. Nainital is a beautiful hill station in the foothills of *Himalayas*. We took a train from Delhi to Kathgodam. From Kathgodam, we hired a local guide, who also provided a Jeep for us. His name was Aarav. He was tall and handsome. By face, he didn't look like a guide as he was speaking English fluently. He took us to Nainital via road. It was raining during the time of our journey, so there were very few people on the roads and shops were closed.

We were stopped a kilometer short of Nainital due to a landslide and we had to cover this last kilometer of our journey on foot. Our guest house was situated near the Naini lake. Surrounded with panoramic seven hills, Naini lake is like heaven on earth. There were pedal boats and rowboats in it. Pedal boats were in three shapes – Duck-shaped, Fish-shaped and standard ones.

As we were tired due to journey, we preferred to take rest that day. Next day, we visited the *Naina Devi* Temple and *Pashan Devi* temple which is situated on the *'Thandi Sadak'* on the other bank of the lake. We enjoyed the walk alongside the lake periphery, covering four kilometers in one day.

Aarav's voice and personality was very charismatic I found myself gazing at him again and again.

In the evening, we planned a night out with a fire camp on the bank of Naini Lake. Aarav warned us and advised us to stay in the guest house. He told us about the wild animals who wandered near the lake at night. He told us the story of a lady who was attacked by the leopard. She was badly injured, lying on the ground, her clothes strewn around her. Leopard attacked this lady in the left side of her head. Her skull was broken. She was breathing but senseless. Soon after, she died.

We all were laughing listening to his tale. We did not take him seriously as we thought he was just making stories to pass time.

The freezing night of winters and chilly winds of the Himalayas made it the perfect time for *bonfire* with friends. All my friends were singing and dancing, having fun. Aarav was sitting near the bonfire, alone. He was smiling, looking at my friends. I was looking at him.

Suddenly one of my friends shouted my name, *"Arushi!"*

Fear laced her voice. She shouted again, this time even more loudly, *"Arushi look back."*

I turned around and what my eyes saw, I cannot describe in words.

A big cat was standing behind me. I was petrified to see the leopard. My heart was thumping so fast, it felt as if it would come out any second. All my friends were shouting and screaming. I was standing still. In a fraction of a second, the leopard lunged at me with its paws. It dug its claws into my legs, I shouted out loudly for help. He tried to drag me near the lake. I was in horrible pain and screaming for help, *"Save me!"*

 "Help!"

"Somebody please help!"

In a flash, Aarav was there for my help. He grabbed the leopard by his tail in an act of raw courage. He was trying to save my life from leopard. The leopard left my leg. I was lying on the ground, my left leg was bleeding badly. I was in tremendous pain. There was *blood dripping* from his mouth.

Now Aarav and the leopard were in front of each other. There was fear in both of their eyes. The leopard came within a meter of where Aarav was standing and let out a huge roar. Aarav roared back. He roared and roared at the leopard and started making the scariest faces in front of leopard. Within a minute, the leopard was on Aarav. He attacked Aarav over and over again with his paws. Aarav was injured but his efforts didn't waver. His head was against the leopard's chest. He was so close to the leopard's chest that he could hear the leopard's heart which I am sure was thumping fast as well.

Suddenly, my friends showed some courage and came with long pieces of wood, and bonfire sticks and tried to hit the leopard's head. When they made loud noises and hit the leopard with the sticks, the leopard released Aarav and ran away into the jungles.

Aarav came near to me, I was still on the ground. He asked me if I was okay. He was bleeding. I could clearly see the scars on his neck - puncture marks of the leopard's claws.

One of my friends made a call to forest department and local police station for reporting this incident. They took us to the nearby hospital for the treatment. There, I got to know that Aarav had a Bachelor's degree in commerce but due to his father ill health, he was doing this local guide's job because he did not want to go to a city for a job as he couldn't leave his father alone in this situation.

After this incident, I *fell in love* with Aarav. He was my life savior and later, he became my life partner. A partner for ever.

"Once romance was only a dream for me,

Without love, life seemed difficult to me,

But then you did appear

All of a sudden, it seemed so clear

I found a soul mate in you

With you, I discovered a new way in life.

Please never break my heart

Never wave your hands for the goodbye.

I wish our love only thrives

I wish it always blooms

I wish for it to never die."

Candle Light Dinner

Aarav came into my life like a flash- all at once, brightly and instantaneously present. After a few months of dating, tonight is the first time Aarav has invited me to his home for dinner. I rang the bell and checked my appearance one last time through my front camera as I waited for him to open the door. Upon entering his apartment, I was surprised to see his house not as messy as I had imagined it to be. He surely must have cleaned up the place before my arrival. He had put on some soft romantic music and was humming to its melody while pouring out our drinks. Strings of mini lights on the wall created the atmosphere of being under the night sky. A sweet fragrance prevailed around the room, probably from the beautiful candles he had decorated the room with.

"Arushi!" He gave a peck on my lips while handing me the glass, making me blush.

He took my hand and led me to the middle of the room to dance. At first, I was a bit hesitant but eventually, I was just swaying to the music that I wasn't even listening to – while my head rested on his shoulder.

Over the course of the evening, we talked, laughed and engaged in friendly banter. Later, we had our dinner, which Aarav had himself prepared for me and I must say *'his cooking skills are quite commendable.'* By the end of the dinner, we had comfortably abandoned our glasses and were directly drinking the wine from the bottle.

It was about 2 am when we settled in bed and decided to watch a movie. We kept laughing and moving closer all through the night. I could see his face and smile, hear his melodious voice which seemed like music to my ears. *We were cuddled up in layers of blankets over us.*

By 5 am, I just couldn't keep my eyes open anymore and I was way too comfortable, curled up next him, the thought of leaving not coming to my mind even once.

And that was the first time I spent the night with Aarav. We did this quite often in the months that followed. And I loved those nights filled with conversation, laughter and him.

"In a dim candle light,

We danced together that night

I felt the warmth & love in your eyes,

Your cheeks went red, you become shy.

Lying in bed, kissing you

Your lips were so sweet,

Your soul was so divine,

Lost in the fire of passion,

I was completely yours, you were completely mine.

At midnight,

I captured a glimpse of your face,

You looked like a goddess in full moon rays,

A beautiful sweet memory,

to remember always."

A Tale Of Destiny

It all started in October 2014. I was a new comer in the music industry and my career was running at the speed of a snail at that time. My friends decided to visit a fair in our small city, *Nangal*. While we were enjoying the fair, I saw a *'fortune teller stall'*. My friends told me that what these psychics predict actually comes true. So, out of curiosity, I went there. I told myself I wasn't going to give him any hints, and I definitely wasn't going to take anything the Psychic said too seriously.

"Come in, girls." A female voice called out.

"You have an appointment?" She asked.

We shook our heads, 'No'.

"Okay, who wants to go first?" She gestured at one of her cabin that was dark inside.

"Can't we go together?" I asked.

She smiled slightly and shook her head. "No. You must go alone." Every sentence she said sounded very spooky, adding to her mystical appeal. It only enhanced my experience.

"Arushi, you go first", my friends said.

She led me into the cabin and closed the door slowly with a devilish grin. *'She's really legit!'* I thought to myself as the door creaked spookily, as if on cue. In the corner of the room, I noticed apothecary jars filled with different colored crystals and powders, a deck of tarot cards, a cat and a crystal ball.

"Hold out your hands." Her eyes closed and she meditated for a second before saying, *"You're a very positive person."*

I nodded and she continued.

"You like to be happy and you seek happiness. You also try to help others as much as you can but fate is not helping you. You are struggling with your career, music."

I nodded again. I was so shocked at that time. All that she is saying is true!

"You have a trip coming up, To Goa. Have you planned that yet?" She asked, gazing into her crystal ball.

I said, *"No."*

"You will. That's where you'll meet him, your soul mate, one who will change your fate." She said again. This time, even her cat nodded and made the sound of meow.

At this point, I had never even thought of going to Goa. Punjab was all I knew. My mind is filled with thoughts. Why will I be going to Goa? Why will a Punjabi singer go to Goa? Goa is all about foreigners, English, French, Portuguese and their local language. I'll see if that even happens.

"Alright, we are done." she said.

I was shocked. Done already? It hadn't even been ten complete minutes.

When we exited the cabin, all my friends were in curiosity so as to know what she had told me. We were all looking at each other.

The psychic lady put on a mysterious smile and asked, "Aren't you forgetting something?"

"Ah...payment..." I rasped.

"Oh, right, right," I muttered, fumbling for my wallet.

500 rupees (10$ approximately) for 10 minute prediction not a bad business at all.

Few weeks later, I got a call from my sponsors planning a concert in Goa. I was shocked.

Damn, half of her predication was already right!

So now, it's concert time, and we are on the way to Goa. At practice, my personal assistant, Garima, told me about the leading male singer of the concert, Aarav. She told me that Aarav is a famous name in the music industry. He was popular among the youth. There he arrived, half an hour late. The sponsors introduced us.

It was Garima who greeted him first.

"You did not change. Even today you are half an hour late", I smiled and said to Aarav.

"Arushi, is it you? But let me tell you. You are completely changed." Aarav replied with a smile of his own.

"Ma'am, do you know each other?" Garima asked.

I looked in Aarav eyes and said, "Yes. We were classmates in our school time."

"Once I had proposed her but she rejected my proposal because she thought she was beautiful and I was just a simple looking guy", Aarav told Garima.

Our concert was a big hit and after the concert, Aarav and I became good friends again. However, it is out of my understanding as to why he wanted to be friends with a calm struggling girl, who had rejected him in 10th standard. We started messaging back and forth for weeks, updating each other on what we were up to. He was very popular and so he had to travel to different states for the shows, his life was so much more exciting than mine. I was also getting shows but not the huge, big budget ones. Whenever I found the time, I messaged him or made a call. Aarav was always there, messaging me calling me and helping me in passing out time. With every message and call, I started liking him more and more and hoped that he had started to feel the same.

After a year of messaging and calling, it so happened that we were going to be in Delhi for the same show (*call it fate*) and we met again. Our duo was a big hit and so was the concert that night.

After the concert, I realized that I definitely liked him and it turned out that the feelings were mutual.

Now came the tricky part. I lived in Nangal. Aarav lived in Delhi. Neither of us had ever been in a long distance relationship before, but we were willing to put it to test. We ignored all the odds against us and hoped it wouldn't be an issue down the road of our prosperous relationship.

The first time I flew into Delhi after that, for one of my concerts, I found Aarav standing outside the airport with a bouquet of roses and a sign that read "Arushi Sharma". Like one of those drivers that pick you up, you know the kind. As I stared at him in awe, he flipped the sign around and it said, *"Will you be my girlfriend?"* This is the most *'CUTEST'* thing which I see in my whole life.

"Yes, I will!" I replied.

We've been a couple ever since.

We have been going out for 4 years now and our relationship consists of planned visits and many flights. Being in a Long Distance Relationship is not that easy. Long distance is not for everybody. It's a lot of work and it will test your relationship in ways that doesn't happen in normal relationships. We've come to appreciate the small things and not think twice about fighting over things that don't matter. We cherish every moment we get to spend together.

In my heart, I knew I had found the one when all the miles in between didn't mean a thing and realized distance really does make the heart grow fonder.

Soon we will plan our marriage.

But the thing is that, *"Anybody can fall in love whether he is near or far away from you. As love knows no reason, no boundaries, no distance. What Love knows is to love each other, to put a smile on each other face."*

Destiny always makes it work, if it's meant to be.

"If I could have all the time in the world,

You know what I would do;

I would touch your lips and kiss you,

I would hold your waist and hug you,

I would come in your dreams,

And eat strawberry ice cream with you,

I would see through your soul,

And feel the warmth of love with you,

I would spend all my time,

Together,

Always with you!"

Simple Arranged Marriage

When love happens before the arranged marriage, it is called *Love cum arranged* marriage, but what if it happens after the arranged marriage?

I will prefer to call it *arranged love marriage!*

I was born and bought up in the village *Daghour* in Punjab while Arushi was from the city *Una* (Himachal Pradesh). When the question of our respective careers and jobs arose, both of us had to choose a place other than the one where we used to live in. Arushi found her place of work in the one of the finest cities of India, Chandigarh while I started my career in Ludhiana, then moved to Jalandhar and finally I shifted to Delhi, thinking that I needed to experience the night life and of the capital city of India

Everything was going exactly as I had planned. After almost a year of fun, adventures and a few good parties in Delhi, one fine morning, my parents called me. My father told me that, "We are going to meet your *'to be bride'* and her family tomorrow".

His words left me stunned. This was not I had planned my life. I felt my head start spinning.

The next evening, my father called me again, telling me that they had met the girl and her family and found her to be a very lovely person. My father convinced me that she was a girl who was the perfect match for me. Finally, due to the pressure they were putting on me, I decided to talk to her on call. My mother arranged her phone number for me.

When I called her, stupidly, the first thing I asked her was her name.

"Arushi." She had replied in a melodious voice.

It was a formal chat with brief introduction about each other, I didn't talk much. This is how our arranged love story began.

Next day, Arushi called me and introduced me to her sister. She was about to leave for Chandigarh from home.

Days passed and we had started talking frequently. Soon, both of us decided to move one step forward and informed our parents that we are willing to marry each other.

Both of our families were happy at that time but my father asked me again, *"Aarav, are you sure? The two of you haven't even met yet."*

It was surely a yes from both of us but I still decided to go and meet Arushi in Chandigarh.

So I booked my flight tickets and flew to Chandigarh the very next day. We met at one of my cousin's place but we didn't talk much. From there, we went out to Elante Mall to meet her friends. After that, I dropped Arushi at her rented apartment and came back. It felt a little strange because unlike our phone conversations, we hadn't talked to each other much. The next day we went to Arabic Infusion for lunch with her friends. It was like our first date. There, we talked in the group but didn't get the chance to directly talk to each other. After spending some time together, I dropped her and went back to my cousin's house. The next day, I flew back to Delhi.

It was a yes from both the sides.

Meanwhile, back at home, our families started planning for our wedding. Both families met, decided the dates and informed us about them.

I planned my next trip to my home town, *Daghour* but with a small twist. This time the route was via Chandigarh and yes, we met again, this time without her friends. We went for lunch and also did some shopping. Three days later, we met on our *Engagement.* The first vow, where we exchanged rings and our families became happier. Then things happened pretty fast, we met whenever there was an opportunity, even when we were living so far from each other.

Our arranged love marriage story was just like a regular story. Not much tales, without much hype, a simple traditional wedding, inviting our close friends, family and others. We never got a chance to think about a dream wedding, a destination wedding or a special wedding. The wedding was planned for February and we had become friends, partners and were living together in our own virtual world. Every single planning required for the marriage, we discussed and then took the decisions. That was the first change. Some decisions which were supposed to be taken and made a practice happened before marriage and yes, a boy and a girl became a man and a woman on *14th February 2014*. That was the day we married each other, our Story took a twist from there.

It's been close to two years now. We kept our promises to each other and are living our life in our ways. We fight, we quarrel, we have fun, we travel, we work, we live and we stay together the same way we stood on that day, the day we took the vow.

'The day when we became one!'

"My heartbeat skips

Whenever my name came on your lips.

You're my endless love

Without you, there's no dawn, no dusk,

You're pretty, cute, gorgeous and charming

I still can't find a perfect word for you, Darling!

You're my cutest little angel,

Emotions, feelings or intensive caring,

You're perfect for me from every angle.

Your big black eyes warm me up and calm me down,

I have begun to fall in love with you completely."

Love Letter

Hey Sparkle,

Can you believe we are completing the 7th year of our relationship? It feels so surreal. I am truly blessed to have you in my life. I adore and love you so much. One day you just walked into my world and everything seemed to fit perfectly. Life is so much more beautiful now. You are the most incredible person that I have ever encountered. Thank you for taking me as your partner in embarking on this beautiful journey of life. I want you to know that I love, appreciate, trust, honor, praise, and worship you with all of my being. I commit, submit and devote all of myself to you and you only. With you by my side, I can solve the most difficult puzzles of life. The love that we share is priceless. Your happiness inspires my happiness.

Arushi, you are the key to my heart. You are my other half, my soul mate. I still remember the day when you accepted my proposal and let me call you mine. You don't believe this but you've managed to take away my breath from the first day we met. I got fascinated to your big blue eyes and perfect, luscious lips. The way I feel when I lie down with you, your arms wrapped around me, holding me like I'm your baby, I never feel less or more when I am with you; you always make me feel needed.

I wish I could wake up every day next to you and see your beautiful face the first thing in the morning. I'm so thankful that you came in my life. You bring out so much in me that I'm just beginning to see. It's like when we are together, the rest of the world disappears, and nothing else matters but us. I hope I feel this way forever. I want to spend the rest of my life loving you with everything I have. Do you know how long I have waited to have someone like you in my life?

You are the sunshine of my life. With you, I feel the happiness every man seeks. It wasn't luck that brought us together, it was fate. You came as a blessing to me. You know, it is strange how I had to go through so many bad situations before you came into my life. I guess it is really true when they say good things come to those who wait because I've waited for someone like you all my life and you really are the best thing that has ever happened to me.

I see you in the stars every time I look up at the sky. You are the song birds sing every morning. You are like the rainbow, filling up my life with bright and cheerful colors. You are everywhere, really.

I just want you to know that I am very fortunate to have you in my life.

I love you and I can't wait to meet you at the altar where we finally hold each other's hands and become one. It will be God's greatest reward.

With love

Aarav.

"You are the reason, why I smiled

A special tone in my heart you dialed,

You fill my world with hope,

You've changed my life,

You understand my emotions

You read my thoughts

You take away all of my heart's droughts.

You are the person who always knows

Whenever life throws its blows

You listen to everything with ease,

And I no longer feel distraught or teased

You wiped my tears whenever I cried.

Your love stood the test of time

I am so lucky to have you in my life

You are the reason why I smiled

Thank you for making me yours and becoming mine."

A Chocolate Kiss

It had been a little less than a year of us being in a long distance relationship. Over its course, we had indulged in the conversations around the topic of kissing, but neither of us was really in a rush to do anything. *I strongly believe that kissing is one of the most intimate ways of expressing our personal emotions and feelings for somebody.* It is the most important aspect of a relationship and romance. But at the same time, I was never really got nervous or excited about it simply because I wasn't waiting around for him to swoop in and kiss me. I knew it would happen in its own course of time.

Aarav lived in Delhi, while I was completing my studies in Jaipur during that time. On one of his official trips, he was supposed to come to my city and so we planned to go on our first date on that *Friday.* I was very excited to see him and had worn a wine colored off-shoulder dress that came up to my knees. While waiting for him, I was browsing my phone when I suddenly looked up and saw him standing across me. *In a button-down red shirt underneath a black blazer, slacks and sexy glasses, he managed to take my breath away.*

"Arushi, Sorry to keep you waiting. I'm so glad to see you." He hugged me softly and handed me a small bunch of *orchids.*

As we went into the restaurant bar, he pulled the chair out for me, behaving like a proper gentleman. I was still feeling a bit shy but as the evening progressed, I felt myself *shedding my inhibitions.* We talked about our families, what we liked and disliked, our future plans and much more. Conversation and laughter were freely flowing.

After a couple of drinks and fine dinner, we moved out of the restaurant. As we strolled along the streets of Jaipur, he had his arm around my waist and I felt so secure. In between the conversation, he offered me a chocolate. His gestures made me blush. We reached the end of the road and turned into a narrow street of terraced houses. Everything was very still and empty.

It might've been around 10 in the evening. The cool breeze of the night made me shiver.

Aarav suddenly stopped and put both his arms around me, pulling me closer. I felt his warm breath on my neck, making shivers run down my spine. His face inched closer to mine and my *heartbeat quickened.* I felt a spurt of courage and put my hands on his chest. I closed my eyes and leaned in. Then, we kissed. It felt like the most extraordinary kiss in the world. It was passionate, yet soft. We were devouring each other. A small piece of chocolate with caramel on my lips made it a very silky smooth type of kiss.

"Extremely Pleasurable!" He whispered to me and feeling my cheeks heat up, I buried my face in the crook oh his neck.

It went on for two hours. He was delicious, dominant, uninhibited and confident. He gave me several orgasms and enough saliva to get me damp in several places on my body just by touching and kissing.

I was aroused but my lips hurt, aching because of the stubble on Aarav's face and yet, I was yearning for more of those amazing wild kisses. We ended up a little messy. But till then I knew a *beautiful memory* was going to be forever etched in my life. After this incident, we kissed each other several times on the numerous occasions we met but I can never forget our first kiss.

"With a drop of Chocolate on your lips

I become an addict,

Do you know which one was our best kiss?

When I licked your coffee stained lips

Explored your mouth with my tongue

Licking your chocolate covered teeth,

I closed my eyes,

In a few moments, I was in paradise,

Our lips synced together like molten chocolate

Ah' what a delight

It was a soft emotional touch

This Chocolate tastes so pure

This chocolate is so nice

It is a mixture of devotion and divine

This Chocolate is so sweet,

This Chocolate is mine."

A Cup of Tea

During the final year of my college, one night I was finishing one of the papers due the next day when my phone rang. I was surprised as it was quite late and the call was coming from an unknown number. The guy on the other side started talking immediately and it was pretty easy to figure out that he had dialed a wrong number. He sounded half asleep and half heartbroken. I couldn't bring myself to tell him the truth and kept talking to him. After some time, it was inevitable for him to realize that the person he was talking to was not the same person he had thought he was talking to.

"Who are you?" He exclaimed in an accusatory tone.

"Don't get mad, please! I am Arushi and you sounded so sad, I wanted to help lighten your pain." I said.

"Well, Arushi, I don't think I can blame you completely as it was my fault too." He sighed.

And then we continued talking, my assignment completely abandoned. He told me that he had meant to call his ex-girlfriend, who had stopped answering his texts and calls, and in the excitement of having the call picked up, he didn't stop to think that it was actually somebody else who had answered.

An hour later when we were about to hang up, he finally asked, *"So, shall I just keep hitting re-dial?"* and so, I gave him my number.

That is how Aarav and I talked for the first time.

The session of calls continued and two months later, we decided to meet. It so happened that both our colleges were in the North Campus, so we met in the evening after our classes in a coffee shop.

After the courteous greetings, we sat downed and ordered tea. *I smiled to myself at the irony of ordering tea in a coffee shop but we are Indians; it is our inherent right to drink tea in every occasion possible.* However, the irony did little to cut the tension looming at our table. Aarav sat like a statue, saying nothing for the first time since I had known him. I didn't know what to do. The sandwiches and tea were cold by now and I was contemplation whether all of this was just a bad decision. Suddenly, Aarav broke his silence and asked the waiter for some salt.

I gave him a *perplexed* look.

He replied in a shivering voice, *"I'd like to put it in my tea."*

I was aghast and all I could do was stare at him. His face turned red.

He put the salt in his tea and drank it.

"Why would you drink tea like this?" I asked him, curiously.

He replied, *"My mom used to love drinking her tea like this. She is no more now. So, every time I drink salty tea, it reminds me of her, how she worked hard and took care of me after my father's death. I miss my mom so much."* Tears welled up in his eyes but he controlled his emotions. I was deeply touched by his wordings.

The salt turned out to be the *ice-breaker* and after that, conversation flowed like water between us. This was the beginning of our beautiful story.

We continued to date and I soon found that Aarav actually was a man who fulfilled all my demands. He was the prince charming who had tolerance, a kind heart and most importantly, he was careful.

Years later, we got married and lived a happy life together. Each and every time, whether in the morning or in the evening, whenever I made tea for Aarav, I used to add some salt in his tea, as I knew that's the way he liked it.

After 45 years, Aarav passed away.

One day, while cleaning his cupboard, I found a letter in his personal diary. A letter addressed to me, in which he said, "Hey Boo Bear, please forgive me, forgive the lie I told you my entire life. Believe me, Arushi, this was the only lie I said to you in my whole life-the salty tea. Remember the first time we met? I was so nervous at that time, I had actually wanted some sugar, but instead, said salt. It was hard for me to change and so, I just went ahead with it. I hadn't thought at that time that we would get married one day. I tried to tell you the truth many times in my life, but I was too afraid to do that, as I had promised not to lie to you about anything. Because I'm dying now so, I'm afraid of nothing and that is why I am telling you the truth now: I don't like the salty tea, what a bitter taste it has. Yet, I have no remorse for anything I've done for you. Having you with me is the biggest happiness of my life. If I get to live for the second time, I would still want to know you and have you for my whole life, even if I would have to drink the salty tea again."

Teardrops fell on the letter as I continued to cry, clutching it to my chest.

Some days later, I went to the same coffee shop and ordered a tea with some salt. A couple arrived and asked me, *"How does the salty tea taste?"*

I smiled and said, *"It's the sweetest."*

"Over a cup of tea,

One evening she asked me,

What is love?

I replied

Love is sweet, love is nice,

Love knows no limits,

Love is the expression of heart and mind.

Love is caring, love is sharing,

Love is when you smile,

Love is the cutest thing in your life.

Love is soft, love is hot,

To love is to never lose hope

Love is the mixture of glory and pride."

Old Age Love

Aarav and Arushi were married for 63 years. Though Aarav was 86 and Arushi was 84 years old, their relationship seemed so fresh and young – *a bond of true love*.

I'm Saksham Vashisht, a doctor by profession, I first met the senior couple when Aarav uncle brought aunt Arushi in a wheelchair to the hospital for a routine check-up of her disease.

Who says that only young lovers can spread the fragrance of love?

I found this old couple a sight to see – they looked ever so in love, always smiling at each other, eyes filled with adoration for the other, gazing at each other (I wonder if they could see each other clearly with those weaken eyes) and had an aura of understanding around them.

"Do you remember our first motorbike ride?" asked uncle Aarav while pushing his wife's wheelchair.

"Yes, I do. You were driving too fast that day," She replied. You could make out the signs of contentment on her face as she had complete trust and faith in her husband.

Aunt Arushi was suffering from Paralysis, and her old age made the matters worse. She needed regular treatment. After a few weeks of treatment, she started improving; however, she still needed to visit the hospital frequently for routine check-ups.

Even though uncle Aarav himself wasn't fit enough and age had weakened his body, he was still strong mentally and wouldn't make any compromises for the love of his life. He had to travel great distances and spend a lot of money, yet he refused to take her to just any hospital as he only wanted the best treatment for his love.

As time passed by, the serious effects of the disease and failing treatment started showing on aunt Arushi's health. Yet, I could see the love and respect they had for each other.

Uncle Aarav would just remain *quiet* and aunt Arushi would read her husband's love through his *silent eyes*. They didn't need any words to express their love, as true love needs no language.

When I hadn't seen the couple for a few days, I called up uncle Aarav. I know it was a bit unethical but I still made the call.

It was uncle Aarav on the phone and he told me that my aunt Arushi had passed away a week back, due to nervous system breakdown.

Uncle Aarav conveyed all this in a shaky voice to me as he broke into sobs. It was the first time in the five months that I had known him that he cried or showed any helplessness. He cried on the phone endlessly and uncontrollably. It was the first time his voice indicated defeat and pain, which all this time he had concealed in order to give courage to his wife.

He told me how empty his house and heart felt, and how he couldn't sleep nor eat. His wife was no longer by his side – but he mentioned how much he still loved her and wished for her soul to rest in peace.

It made me think about how people cope with such a great loss, and how do they gather the strength and courage to carry on with life. After going through their story of love – *the beautiful bond and silent understanding*, it made me realize that there's always another side to a story, more than what meets the eye. True love isn't necessarily a domain of young couples and known only by public display of affection. True love needn't be overtly expressive. It is the unconditional love lovers yearn for. To love someone unconditionally in simple words means to love a person without any conditions. You love them as they are, just as they were before, and just as they will be in the future.

That's because people change all the time, so if you love a person unconditionally, you will love them even if they become something you don't agree with, or even if they become old and sick – isn't it?

True love is unconditional love when you love a person for their innermost essence – their soul. You see the person and love them for who they are. You appreciate and be grateful. In that, contentment lies.

"If love is a tragedy,

Then love is sweet too,

If love is cruel,

Then love is pure too,

If love is painful,

It also makes two souls one.

If love is a poison,

Don't worry, there are many more opportunities too.

If love is an unexplainable question,

Then love is an ample answer too,

If love is a misunderstanding,

Then check again

Maybe, Love is misunderstood by you."

Miss Beautiful

Everything around her felt like a blur as she left the doctor's room. His words kept ringing in her head, *"Arushi, you are suffering from stage-four cancer."* Tears were freely flowing from her eyes. It was difficult for a 19 years old to comprehend that her time on this beautiful planet was so short and about to be over soon.

She reached her home and locked herself in her room. She was exhausted from crying and did not want to talk to anybody. She wanted to be alone with her thoughts. There was a shower of text messages from her friends, each wishing her a happy birthday, but she ignored all of them; she wasn't happy and she didn't feel like celebrating. She had forgotten that it was her birthday. There felt like no reason to celebrate life when it was so close to its end and so, being taken cared by her mother, stuck in her own house was what became of her life. She stopped going outside.

Days passed and her condition got worse. She became very *frail and weak.* But she was tired of staying at home and wanted to go out for once. So, with her mother's permission, she took a stroll to the nearby market. Her feet themselves stopped in front of the book store she had spent countless afternoons sitting in. As she peered inside, there was a new guy standing at the counter, probably of the same age. She knew it was *love at first sight*. She quickly walked into the book store, not looking at anything else but this guy.

She walked up to the front desk where he was sitting.

The guy looked up and asked *"Can I help you?"*

The smile he flashed Arushi made her swoon and she thought it to be the most beautiful smile she had ever seen. Her dream boy was standing in front of her. She thought about kissing him, hugging him and just before her thoughts could wander any farther, her doctor's haunting words came back to her.

"Yes. I would like to buy *'For Someone Special'* by Yogesh Sharma." She picked the book and gave him the money for it.

"Would you like me to wrap it up for you?" he asked, smiling. *Oh, God!* His cute smile again.

Her own smile came up as she nodded and he went to the back.

He came back with the wrapped book and gave it to her. She took the book and walked out of the store. She went home and from then on, she went to that store every day and bought a book, and the guy wrapped it for her. She took the book home and put it in her bookshelf.

At last, she decided to tell this guy about her feelings. She gathered up the courage and went to the store. She bought a book like she did every day and once again the guy went to the back of the store and came back with it wrapped. She took it and when the guy was busy in attending another customer, she left her phone number with her name on the desk and walked out of the store quickly.

After two days, the guy called on Arushi's number.

Her mother picked up the phone and said, *"Hello?"*

"Is this Arushi? I'm Aarav from book store."

"No!" her mother replied and started to cry. She said, "You don't know? Arushi passed away yesterday."

There was silence on both sides afterwards. Aarav hung up without another word.

Later in the evening, Arushi's mother went into her room and was surprised to see so many wrapped books on her bookshelf. She picked one up and sat down on the bed to open it. As she turned the cover to the first page, she saw a handwritten poem on it.

"You are the most beautiful,

With a smile that brightens up your face,

I am so lucky to have you,

You take my breath away.

You are perfect for me in every single way.

You are so lovable,

Your personality is adorable,

I want to kiss you,

I want to take care of you, each and every day.

You are so special,

Your eyes to your heart are a maze,

Keeping me always lost in your gaze

I want to stay with you,

I love you forever & always."

Hi. It's me, Aarav. I think your eyes are really beautiful. Would you like to go out with me? Love Aarav.

Arushi's mother unwrapped another book...

Again, the same lines were written on the front page of the book.

One more book unwrapped…

Same lines again…

A Dream of a Sprinter

From her childhood, Arushi liked participating in race and sprinting competitions. The anticipation just before the start, the adrenaline rush while running, the euphoria of winning with sweat beads all over her face drove her on. She now had only one dream for herself, the dream of winning a Gold medal for her country in sprinting at international level. She had initially started winning almost every year in her school's Sports Day Competitions. In her 10th Class exams, she stood first with 80% marks but instead of choosing science for her further studies, she chose humanities so that she could continue to work on her dream. She trained harder and better with each passing day. Soon enough, her dedication paid off and she won the State Level Tournament. Now, the next step was Nationals. However, destiny had other plans for her.

 Arushi's father died in a road accident. Her father, who was a big support for her, was no more there to cheer up his daughter.

Arushi's life changed dramatically. Her mother fixed her marriage with an electrical engineer, Aarav, the proposal brought by some distant relative. Even after numerous protests, her mother did not waver, saying she was incapable of sustaining the both of them on her own and wanted a good life for Arushi. After her marriage, Arushi *lost her will* and thought it was all over for her. How would a man, engineer by profession, understand her dream and support her for achieving it? Even though it broke her heart, she decided to forget her dream and move on in her life.

Months later, on one of their trips to Arushi's mother's house, Aarav saw her medals and certificates and asked his mother in law about this. She told him that Arushi had been a sprinter before their marriage and her dream was to win a medal for India. Later in the evening, Aarav told Arushi that he will support her in achieving her goal. He even told her that they can plan their family later, after Arushi achieves her dream. Arushi's joy knew no bounds. That day, her dream came back alive just because of her husband, Aarav. She again started her practice. She participated in National level 100m and 200m sprint and won gold medals in both. Now, she was eyeing the International level race.

And just when Arushi thought she was very much near to finally achieving her dream, life took a strange turn. While she was travelling to Chandigarh for one of her tournaments, she met with a major accident. The accident was so brutal doctors had to amputate both her legs.

Arushi was shattered because it was only then that she realized just how passionate she felt about her dream. She was heart-broken. Aarav was still with her. He was the only person who was still supporting her. With each passing day, Arushi's optimism about life sunk more and more. Then one day, Aarav came up with *prosthetic legs*. He was still watching that dream of receiving a medal. He lifted her spirits and it was only then that Arushi decided to do it again.

Arushi began to learn how to walk again and it took her 8 months to do so. Aarav arranged for a physiotherapist and physiatrist for her so that she could recover and feel normal again. Despite her limitations, Arushi pushed herself physically and mentally to succeed. Aarav left his *job and mortgaged* their house so that he could provide world class facilities to Arushi. He even arranged for an international coach. Slowly but steadily, she started participating in the usual activities of her peers which other athletes do, swimming, biking and soccer alongside "able-bodied" athletes. Motivation of her husband and her amazing spirit and drive helped compensate for the portion of her body she was missing.

After so much of hard work, finally the day for which both of them had been waiting for, arrived. *She was selected for an international event.* Both Aarav and Arushi were happy on that day.

However, when Arushi reached the venue, she realized with surprise that she was the only athlete wearing wooden legs. The rest of the athletes had metal shock-absorbent legs that she didn't even know existed. Also, they all had at least one normal leg. Instead of *deterring her determination though*, this forced Arushi to push herself harder to succeed. And succeed she did – *she not only won the gold medal, she also broke an International record in doing so.*

Her dream came true and the reason is the only person who never lost his faith in her. It was a proud moment for her, receiving a gold medal while the national anthem of her country was playing in the background. That is what she had dreamt all her life. She was finally at peace.

After receiving her medal, Arushi said few words at the presentation ceremony:

"All I have achieved today is because of that one person who stood by me during the most difficult period, the man who has loved me selflessly. He kept motivating me; he never let me lose hope. His love taught me to be strong and face every situation boldly. He helped me grow. There was a time when I felt lost about my future but he brought back the confidence in me, made me who I am today. It was his constant encouragement and support that I made it to this International event. I learnt that if the love is true, it would bring out the best in you, make the best of you. And that's how my life changed- from an immature, emotional, low-confidence looser to a mature, grown up, smart woman who believes in herself now and can achieve anything in life. Thank you Aarav, the spirit of my life, the sun of my world."

"Oceans apart,

Your eyes drink me,

The love in them makes them shine,

Your eyes that lean

So, close to mine.

We have long been lovers,

We know the range

Of each other's moods

And how they change;

But when we look

At each other

Then we feel

How little we know;

The spirit eludes us,

Timid and free-

Can I ever know You,

Or you know me?"

Last Birthday

After the chilling and bleak winter, spring season arrived and along with itself, brought Arushi's birthday as well. It was her 21st birthday and all the more special because it was the first time she was celebrating it with someone else since her parent's death. As the sun sank lower in the sky, giving way to the *crimson and orange* hues in the horizon, Arushi sat beside her window, waiting for Aarav. She looked at the clock and sighed. She wondered whether Aarav will come or not? It was her first birthday with Aarav. In these six months, they became such lovebirds who hardly ever stayed apart.

The doorbell rang. It was Aarav; smiling and holding a bouquet of red and white roses, just the way she loved. He hugged her and planted a kiss on her forehead, wishing her happy birthday. Then, he took her upstairs to the roof as there was supposed to be a meteor shower that night. As they sat cuddled together on the rooftop while stargazing, they took a trip down the memory lane. From the first day they met, to the first time they kissed. From the long drives they went to, to the early morning breakfasts they had together, they talked about everything. Later, they had a candlelight dinner with their favorite red wine.

After the dinner, both of them sat beside each other gazing at the sky. Cool breeze, silent environment and dozens of shooting stars creating the perfect romantic situation. It felt like the perfect evening to Arushi.

She turned to look at Aarav but found him already staring at her, his eyes shimmering with love. She felt overwhelmed; Aarav was more than anything she could ever ask for.

Looking into each other's eyes, Aarav softly held Arushi's face in his hands and just when she closed her eyes and was about to lean in, her phone rang.

She cursed the phone for breaking the moment, but nevertheless, excused herself to take the call.

She answered the call and a resonant voice came from the other end.

"Hi Ma'am Do you know Aarav?"

"Yes", she replied.

The voice continued. *"I'm afraid the gentleman has met with a fatal accident and has succumbed to it. I am calling from police station. We got your number from his smartphone. Kindly come to police station and identify his body."*

Suddenly everything became black for Arushi! *"But how is that possible? This cannot happen!"* she told herself. Her voice choked and she could hardly speak. Somehow, she gathered herself and said, *"But he is with me."*

To assure herself, she looked around but nobody was there. Phone fell from her hand. Everything came to a standstill. A quiver ran through her body. She was feeling so helpless. She looked so lost! She was started sweating now.

She ran towards the dining table. Two wine glasses were there but only one was empty. Also, there was a plate with food in it.

She was shivering and crying at the same time. She smashed the wine glass on the floor and screamed. This could not be true. Aarav, her Aarav, was gone. With just one phone call, her whole world came crashing down.

It was the spirit of Aarav that came to her the last time to wish her on her birthday.

At the police station, the policemen handed over Aarav's personal diary to Arushi. His last words for her were…

"If I was to give you a gift,

It would be a smile,

Every morning, you wake up with it

And go after life.

It would be a care,

For your every problem,

I will always be there.

It would be a hope,

To break all those negative shackles,

And achieve your goals.

It would be affection,

With lots of hugs, kisses and selfless attentions.

It would be a love,

Pure, chaste and always together

Our love is such a thing which would last forever.

Just close your eyes and count till two,

I will forever be with you."

Misunderstanding

When Arushi first came to Mumbai, Aarav was the first guy she met. He had been a struggling dancer and actor. They found an instant connection with each other. They were drawn towards each other's personalities. Since both of them were struggling to establish their names in the entertainment industry, they decided to work together in a dance group. While working together, their bond strengthened and soon enough, they fell in love.

Eventually, their hard work paid off and they became famous personalities of the entertainment industry. After two years of dating, Arushi and Aarav decided to tie the knot and get married. For both of them, life was running smoothly, full of love and care.

Around a year later, one day while driving by a famous restaurant in his car, Aarav saw Arushi with his best friend, *Abhishek*. Holding each other's hands, they were smiling together. He was on his way to the airport, going to the USA for a concert, he ignored this and went away.

After a week, he came back home in the evening. Nobody was there. He tried to call Arushi, but her phone was switched off. When the clock *struck 11*, a car stopped in front of Aarav's house. When

Aarav looked outside from his room's window, he saw Arushi with Abhishek. Abhishek dropped her and went off.

When Arushi entered the room, she saw Aarav sleeping in bed. She was unknown to the fact that Aarav was pretending to sleep. She changed her dress and went to sleep next to Aarav. In the middle of the night, Aarav woke up and checked Arushi's phone calls details. He was shocked to see Abhishek's name in the phone call history. She was calling Abhishek 7-8 times daily from the past few days. Aarav was broken from inside, he felt devastated his heart could not believe that Arushi was cheating on him. His heart and mind were in discomfort and in this discomfort, the next day, he left his home.

Before leaving, he wrote a letter to Arushi in which he revealed that he knew about her relationship with Abhishek. He wrote about how he had seen them together, smiling and holding each other's hands. He wrote that he did not wish to come between the two of them. He was feeling cheated. He wrote that he was leaving the house and quitting the relationship.

After reading all this, Arushi broke down miserably. A misunderstanding had taken her husband away. She was pregnant with his baby and was planning a surprise for him with Abhishek. Also, Abhishek's sister was a doctor who was looking after her during this pregnancy period. She had met Abhishek in a restaurant to plan a surprise for Aarav and on the day Abhishek had dropped her at home, she had been visited his sister's nursing home for a check-up and had switched off her phone because phone calls were not allowed there in nursing home.

Due to one misunderstanding, her whole life came crashing down. She tried to search for Aarav but he never came back. Nobody knew where he was. Arushi left the entertainment industry and the city of Mumbai. She opened a *dance school* for small kids in her hometown, *Shimla*.

One day while Arushi was teaching dance in her dance school, she saw someone standing at the auditorium gate. This person was nobody else but Aarav. He came closer to her; he was walking with the help of cane. There were cut marks on his face.

"Arushi" he said.

After seeing Aarav, she couldn't control herself and started weeping loudly.

Aarav held her right hand in his hands and said, *"I am sorry, Arushi!"*

"Where were you? I tried to search and contact you but you never came back. Everything has changed. Without you, I was feeling so incomplete. Where were you when I needed you in my pregnancy? Did you know about our daughter? Deepanki asks about you every day, when will her dad come, when will her father play with her, dance with her and love her? Why? Why? Why did you do this?" she asked Aarav.

Her daughter held her hand, looking innocently into her father's eyes, *"Daddy!"*

Aarav hugged his daughter and kissed her forehead. He was over flown with emotions, his own eyes tearing up.

He told Arushi what had happened to him after leaving their home that day.

"I was walking on the road. My phone rang. It was the doctor on the other side. She told me about your pregnancy reports. Maybe she was trying to contact you but your phone was switched off and so she called on my phone. After hearing that you are pregnant, I felt so happy that in an excitement, I stumbled over a footpath and my phone fell on the road. As I bent to pick it up, a car hit me. I fell unconscious after the accident. The accident was so fatal, I was in comma for five years. The day I gained consciousness, the first word on my lips was

'Arushi'. I started recovering soon. The person who was taking care of me told me about how it had been his car that hit me. He belonged to a rich family and didn't want any media controversy or police case, and so, he decided to help in my medical treatment. I was at his house for five years. He provided me with all medical facilities and the best doctors at home. He said he was sorry and also offered some money as a help. When I start walking initially, I went to our house where I saw a lock on the door. After that, I contacted Abhishek to tell him about all this. He helped me and gave your present address. I have come here only for you."

The three of them kept clutching onto each other, Aarav muttering his apologies, all three weeping.

Finally, the family reunited.

"If you think it's all over after a decade,

Then you are wrong, sweetheart

My love for you will never be fade.

I'm sorry for failing to understand your side,

Give me another chance to hold your hand.

I miss your kiss, I miss your smile,

I miss all those of our silly stupid fights.

I never want you to cry, I can't see you in pain,

I know that I am the only person to be blame.

But believe me, darling, I am changed.

I have learnt from my mistakes,

So, can't we unite once again?

Cause without you, my life is vain."

Fragrance of Her Love

"Good work Aarav! I hope you will do it again for our magazine. Thank you so much for writing your review for this new recipe. Do collect your cheque by Tuesday evening."

It was Mrs. Asha Vasudeva, editor of our magazine.

I'm Aarav, a freelance writer who writes and reviews different recipes for a local magazine. I stay at *Shalimar Bagh* in New Delhi. I have a very sweet and cute girlfriend name 'Arushi'. She has a laundry business, catering to stained and dirty bed sheets and blankets of hospitals and hotels. She loves me very much. We are neighbor as well. Apart from me, she loves perfumes too. She has hundreds of perfumes in her collection. I love the smell of her perfumes.

It all started on the Sunday evening. Arushi had bought a new perfume, and she sprayed a liberal amount of it on her body. She asked me to check it out. I smelled nothing. I pinched the bridge of my nose, then blew it, hard, then took a deep breath through my nostrils, but still there was nothing.

"I can't smell anything." I told her.

I was surprised and so was she. Had I lost my sight or my hearing, I would have been aware immediately, so how was it that I was not even properly conscious of the lack of my sense of smell until the moment with the perfume?

I do know that the smell receptors can also deteriorate with age – half of those over the age of 60 lose at least part of their sense of smell and taste and the condition is known as *Hyposmia*. In another case, the smell does return but in a distorted way, so that everything smells bad. This is known as *Parosmia*. But I was not old enough for this type of condition. I mean, I am just 24. Was it some kind of a serious disease or was it the possibility of a sinus infection? Most people who lose their sense of smell regain it after some time, but some never do.

Next day we consulted a doctor but we did not get the results immediately. He suggested some tests and gave a few medicines. Six week passed and in these six weeks, one thing I got to know was that even if smell is a neglected sense but yet, it was so important for me. You really don't know what you've got until it's gone. Unless you work as a perfumer, or a wine taster, or a freelance writer who writes and reviews different types of recipes, it's not like you rely on it for your daily work.

In the past, I had long problems with my sense of smell. I have suffered from allergies, and also had dodgy sinuses. On a few occasions, when they caused too much pain, I had been offered a minor operation that might correct them, but there is a chance that such a surgery could go wrong and result in the patient losing all sense of smell on a permanent basis. As I was in a profession where your taste and smell buds needed to be perfect, I avoided all those suggestions.

Now, days have passed and my work has started suffering due to this. Food became boring fuel, and wine lost its appeal. I started finding it difficult to write the reviews. I was totally depended on the color and texture of the food to write up its review. Life became miserable. Even my editor Mrs. Asha Vasudeva called me and warned to write correct reviews, powerful ones. I couldn't even smell the perfume of Arushi who stood just next to me. I wondered if this was it forever, that I would never smell anything again.

One day, Arushi called me to her house, something had blocked the drains in her house and she asked whether I could help her with it. When I arrived at her home, I found her holding her nose behind a tissue, telling me the smell of dead rat was overpowering. I smelt nothing, and, being *phobic* of rats, tried to feel relieved. I could not. I helped her to take dead rat out of her house.

She thanked me for this. I was happy that at least there was something where my problem was helping others. After finishing the cleaning, she said she had an idea, *"As you can't smell anything, why don't you help me in my laundry business and I will help you in writing your recipes review, I mean you taste those dishes, I will smelt them and I will tell you the aroma of that dish and then you will write the review for it. Isn't it a good idea? What do you say?"*

"Not a bad idea at all. I can also work well as a pet sitter, especially cats, I do care for them, those stinky cats."

I joined her laundry business. In the day time, I started cleaning the dirty bed sheets and blankets. Though I miss the smell of soap and shampoo, I was happy that I did not need to worry about the bad smell. Also, I was working as a pet sitter for my neighbors. They hired me for their cats and dogs.

In the evening, Arushi helped me in writing reviews of recipes. She tasted the food and then described it to me and after taking the idea, I used write the review.

Between all this, we fell for each other even more. Now, we understood each other far better than we did in the past. One day, I asked Arushi for the dinner date at my home or I should say it was my plan to propose her for the marriage on that day.

My doorbell rang at 7 in the evening, when she arrived. I opened the door and there she was, standing in a red color one-piece dress, her hair curled and left loose, with red lipstick and red nail-paint on her fingers, she was looking absolutely stunning. We hugged each other. Suddenly, something happened. I sneezed.

"Aarav, you sneezed?" Arushi asked me in a surprise.

"Yes, I did." I said.

A second later, I sneezed again. There was a big smile on both of our faces.

"Can you smell something?" she asked again.

It was glorious, her scent — whatever combination of body odor, musk and her perfume, it was not only intoxicating but made me feel like I was on the highest dosage of the most potent psychedelic drug, smell of her perfume turned my head fuzzy and my heart whimsical and everything around me into the brightest of colors. I became mad, running around the house, smelling flowers, clothes, cough medicine, her hair. All smelt glorious.

"Yes, I can smell you. I can smell your perfume", I replied to her in my excitement.

Without wasting a single second, I proposed to her and I knew that our bonding and love was so strong, she would never refuse my proposal. She said yes.

After so many years, my memories have started fading, along with my taste and smell buds but I still can't forget the smell of her 'French perfume'.

"Phiss! Phiss!

And she smiled.

Putting a thin layer of her

Expensive French perfume,

She walked into my room.

She was in my bed,

She was in my head,

I was touching her fingers,

Playing with her hairs,

I could feel her mystic fragrance,

Which was coming from everywhere,

It was her secret potion mixed with odor

It was the smell of her perfume,

Which, forced my soul to feel more."

The Run Away Bride

Every morning followed the same routine for me. Wake up at 6, be ready by 7, have some sausage for breakfast and then bid goodbye to my home. But as we all know, life is full of twists. Similarly, one day I got a surprise of my own.

It was almost a quarter to nine on a Tuesday morning and it was raining outside. I was on my bike, going to office, when I saw a girl standing on the bus stop waiting for the bus. Even though I lived close by, I had never seen her before. I wondered why she was standing there in this rainy weather.

As I was passing by her, she put her hands up in the air and said, *"Stop, please stop!"*

I pulled the brakes of my bike. She was standing in front of me. I was mesmerized by her beauty, her wet hair, her full lips, rain drops were sliding on her cheeks from her forehead. I felt quite nervous and so, I couldn't speak for a moment.

I was thinking about her and suddenly she asked for the lift.

"I need lift. Please drop me at M.G. Road Metro Station, I have an interview and I was waiting for

the bus but it seems that due to the rain, the buses are running late today. I am getting really late for the interview. Please help", she said.

I replied, *"Ok! Come sit, I will drop you."*

While I was driving my bike, both of us sat silently. To break this silence, I started a conversation with her.

"My name is Aarav", I said.

In a low but shrill voice, she said that her name was Arushi.

"So for what kind of a job do you have your interview today?" I asked.

She replied, *"I applied for a job of Accountant, the office where my interview will be held is in Westin Tower."*

It was a short introduction, a formal one. But what attracted me the most was her voice; there was magnetism in her voice because of which I got attracted to her. After a while, we reached at her destination.

Next day, I was passing from the same site where I had met Arushi yesterday. Co-incidentally, she was standing there on the bus stop. She thanked me for the lift I gave and told me that she got the selection because of me. I told her I was glad to be of her help and offered to give her a lift again.

Soon enough, this was a new routine for me. I started waiting at the bus stop daily, to give her a lift. Soon, we started getting closer to each other but we never expressed.

Suddenly, after a period of six months, one day she did not come at the bus stop. I felt upset that day. Next day, I stood at the bus stop again, waiting for her but she did not come. Continuously, I waited for a whole week but she did not come. I was worried and decided to visit her office.

In the office, I met her friend named Kashika. She directly asked me, *"Are you the Aarav she keeps talking about?"*

I was too shocked to speak and just nodded my head.

"I had been trying to find you for a long time but I wasn't able to. I wanted to tell you something about Arushi."

I was frightened and softly asked her to go ahead and tell me.

She told me that from the past few days, Arushi hadn't come to the office. She clarified the whole situation to me about the problem Arushi faced.

Kashika told me that her parents were compelling her to marry somebody she didn't want to.

A loud *'what'* escaped my lips.

She bent her head and said a *'yes'* in a shivering voice.

After thinking for a while, I asked Kashika to help me out. She told me she was ready to help me with all that she could.

Kashika took me to the place where Arushi was getting married. She entered the marriage hall and went to the room where Arushi was getting ready. Arushi sent her relatives out of the room with some excuses and Kashika told her that I was outside, waiting for her. Arushi looked down the window while I was looking up, trying to identify her room, and our eyes met. Her eyes welled up.

In the time being, Kashika took out a rope from her bag and with its help, Arushi came down from the window. The moment she landed in front of me, we said *I love you* to each other with smiling faces. We ran away on my bike. A few minutes later, Kashika also got out of there. After some time, the procession arrived. By the time they found out that Arushi had run away, it was too late.

Arushi and I rushed to the court and soon, Kashika and two of my close friends arrived to act as witnesses.

Drenched in sweat, I asked Kashika, *"Is everything ready?"*

With her face elated with joy, she bowed her neck and nodded a yes.

I told everyone to go inside the court for the main purpose, not wanting to waste any more time. Arushi and I were very scared, but we were very excited and happy from inside as well. Finally, we got married at the right time. I looked in Arushi's eyes and told her that she was going to be mine forever and she hugged me. She cried and told me about how much she loved me but had never said anything. We held each other's hand and walked out of the court and into our new lives.

As the time passes, a new and sweet guest came as a new resident in our house. We felt that our family was complete with his arrival.

After sometime, suddenly Aarushi started remembering her family. We decided to go to them, ask for their forgiveness and have them be a part of our family. We went to her parental house but were very scared as to what would happen now?

Arushi's mother opened the door and saw her grandson with an adoring eyes and asked him, *"Will you not come to Nanny?"*

She asked his name from Arushi and asked us to come inside.

I touched her feet and she blessed me with great affection.

We did it.

Finally, we both felt that our life was successful.

"The way I love you

No one else in this world will do,

The way I hug you,

The way I touch you,

The way I kiss you,

No one else in this world can do.

The way I see you, my angel

The way I feel you, my blessing

The way I dance and the way I romance,

No one else in this world will do.

The way I cry over you,

The way I try for you,

The way I fight but still care for you,

You never know.

For all this, you will miss me one day.

Because the way I love you

No one else in this world will ever do."

How She Fell In My Love

'Dear Arushi,

Your eyes are so big.

I love your hair.

I love your smile.

You are so gorgeous.'

Exasperated, I crumbled the paper in a ball and threw it across the room. I know I can write better than this. I've tried so many times to write to her, to confess my feelings and all my attempts have been futile.

Ever since I joined college, I've had a crush on this really beautiful girl. She has long black hair and stunning brown eyes. She was kind to others and I think what drew me to her the most though was her smile. She had this gorgeous smile, a smile that has the power to light up the room. Whenever she smiled, I felt like the sun had broken through the clouds, I felt a sort of gentle warmth in my heart. I also liked her laugh. I wanted to be the one to make her laugh and to make her smile.

I hadn't known her name initially and one day, I pointed her out in the hall and asked one of my friends about her.

He told me her name was Arushi.

My first thought was that her name is just as beautiful as her.

Slowly, I started noticing things about her. She had a beautiful figure I wish I could describe. She was so kind and patient with people when they made mistakes. I could tell she was very smart too, just from the energy she gave off. She had this kind of confidence radiating from her that I found very appealing. She was a stunning beauty.

But why a stunning beauty like her would ever notice me? Though she has said a few greetings here and there and she knows that my name is Aarav, I doubt she would ever give me any importance in her life. Why would a beauty like her give importance to a person who was creepy, four-eyed, skinny, gigantic, and lanky and like a loser who could not even tell her about his feelings for her. The thing is that I was completely invisible to her. She has got far better options than me. She's out of my league. But there's this weird feeling I have, probably just a delusion, that if I can get to know her somehow, she would like me.

One day, I told one of my friends, Shubham, about it and he told me not to bother asking her out. He said he had himself thought about it but had later figured something out. When I asked him about it, he wouldn't tell. He said he didn't want to reveal this secret, in case it went all over the college. I wasn't planning on blabbing about it. He still wouldn't tell me, so I didn't know whether I should trust him. I mean, he is my friend and I want to give him the benefit of the doubt. But in matters like this, I kind of have to wonder if it's not some trick to keep me away from Arushi so he can try asking her out again. I kept telling myself that it would not be like that. I thought I'm probably over thinking it and I have nothing to worry about.

Situation got worse because there were only few more weeks of college left and it took that long to realize that I loved her. As the final day was coming closer, my heart started pounding and my mind started swirling with emotions. I desperately wanted to tell her about how much I love her. Finally, I decided to confess to her. I decided to tell her in our college fest. I participated in one event and decided to write and read out a poem for her.

The day had come, the fest began and my act was at the very end. The fest was on its peak as everybody was dancing, singing and performing like professionals. I felt a bit nervous. I hadn't ever participated in such kind of fests or programs. I could feel my palms sweating. At last, the moment arrived when my name was announced. I stood on the stage, in front of a modern day youth. Will they like it or not? Who cares? I just want to convey my feelings for Arushi. I closed my eyes, my heart was thumping, and took a long breath. I read the poem with all my heart, love, feelings and emotions.

After reading the poem, I opened my eyes. The crowd was silent. I was afraid. What went wrong? Suddenly, the auditorium was filled with applause. All of them were roaring and shouting, *"Once more! Once more!"*

But my eyes were trying to find someone else. Arushi was not there. I felt sad. I was returning from the fest and just when I reached the campus gate, someone called my name, "Aarav". I turned around it was Arushi.

"I wanted to ask you something." She said.

I nodded, motioning for her to go ahead, too hurt because of her absence to say anything.

"Did you write that poem for me Aarav? Do you really love me?" She asked innocently, looking straight into my eyes.

"I do, Arushi. I really, really do. I could just never muster up the courage to tell you that." I told her the truth, while looking at the ground, too afraid of her reaction.

She came forward and smacked my head.

"You idiot, I love you too. You made me wait so long for this proposal."

My head shot up.

"You do?" I asked, bewildered.

All she did was run up to me and I pulled her into my arms. Just as our lips met, fireworks shot off in the background, signaling the end of college and the start of my love story.

"I don't think she knows

I love her …

From the first day of our college

I have had a crush on her.

When she talks, I watch her lips,

Imagine myself kissing her cheeks.

Her beautiful eyes are bright and deep,

Whenever she smiled, it made my knees go weak.

Her body is perfection, though she denies it,

She looks sexy, gorgeous, charming

With every glance I give,

I don't think she knows how I feel.

Should I tell her or give her a clue?

Because college is to an end soon,

I wish I could have kissed her once,

Just to get the taste of heaven on earth."

23351719R00068

Printed in Great Britain
by Amazon